KU-264-374

Here is
SIMPKIN

Simpkin
ONCE

and Simpkin
TWICE

Y1 T2
Patterned
Lang

S   N

Coventry City Libraries
Schools' Library Service

04013

Red Fox

PET

A Red Fox Book

Published by Random House Children's Books
20 Vauxhall Bridge Road, London SW1V 2SA

A division of Random House UK Ltd
London Melbourne Sydney Auckland
Johannesburg and agencies throughout the world

Copyright © Quentin Blake 1993

3 5 7 9 10 8 6 4 2

First published by Jonathan Cape Limited 1993

Red Fox edition 1995

This book is sold subject to the condition that it
shall not, by way of trade or otherwise, be lent,
resold, hired out, or otherwise circulated without the
publisher's prior consent in any form of binding or
cover other than that in which it is published and
without a similar condition including this condition
being imposed on the subsequent purchaser.

The right of Quentin Blake to be identified as the
author and illustrator of this work has been asserted
by him in accordance with the Copyright, Designs
and Patents Act, 1988.

Printed in Hong Kong

RANDOM HOUSE UK Limited Reg. No. 954009

ISBN 0 09 930230 6

Simpkin NASTY

Simpkin NICE

Simpkin FAST

and Simpkin SLOW

Simpkin HIGH

and Simpkin
LOW

Simpkin
  ROUND and ROUND
      the chairs

Simpkin UP

and DOWN the stairs

Simpkin THIN

and Simpkin FAT

Simpkin THIS

and Simpkin THAT

Simpkin WEAK

and Simpkin STRONG

Simpkin SHORT

and Simpkin LONG

Simpkin SMOOTH

and Simpkin ROUGH

and Simpkin

THAT IS QUITE ENOUGH

Simpkin WARM

and Simpkin CHILLY

Simpkin SENSIBLE

and
SILLY

And

sometimes

when

we

stand

and

call

Simpkin

JUST

NOT

THERE

AT

ALL

Significant Author